The Invisible Bunny
and
The Secret Pony

Look out for more
Magic Molly books

www.holly-webb.com

The girl who talks to animals

Magic Molly

The Invisible Bunny & The Secret Pony

HOLLY WEBB

Illustrated by Erica Jane Waters

SCHOLASTIC

Scholastic Children's Books
An imprint of Scholastic Ltd
Euston House, 24 Eversholt Street
London, NW1 1DB, UK
Registered office: Westfield Road, Southam, Warwickshire, CV47 0RA
SCHOLASTIC and associated logos are trademarks and/or registered
trademarks of Scholastic Inc.

Magic Molly: The Invisible Bunny
First published in the UK as *Molly's Magic: The Invisible Bunny*
by Scholastic Ltd, 2009
Text copyright © Holly Webb, 2009
Illustration copyright © Erica Jane Waters, 2009

Magic Molly: The Secret Pony
This edition published 2013
First published in the UK as *Molly's Magic: The Secret Pony*
by Scholastic Ltd, 2009
Text copyright © Holly Webb, 2009
Illustration copyright © Erica Jane Waters, 2009

The rights of Holly Webb and Erica Jane Waters to be identified as
the author and illustrator of this work have been asserted by them.

ISBN 978 1 407 13547 2

A CIP catalogue record for this book is available from the British Library.

Printed and bound by CPI (UK) Ltd, Croydon, CR0 4YY
Papers used by Scholastic Children's Books are made from wood
grown in sustainable forests.

1 3 5 7 9 10 8 6 4 2

This is a work of fiction. Names, characters, places, incidents and dialogues are
products of the author's imagination or are used fictitiously. Any resemblance to
actual people, living or dead, events or locales is entirely coincidental.

www.scholastic.co.uk/zone
www.holly-webb.com

For Alice, and Annie, who is
not at all like Mrs James...

The Invisible Bunny

Chapter One

The Birthday Party

Molly pulled on her favourite pink jeans, and her T-shirt with the puppies on it. She'd bought it with her pocket money the last time Mum had taken her shopping. The puppies looked so like her friends Star and Stella, the wish puppies, that she hadn't been able to resist it.

Molly smiled at the puppies. She hadn't seen Star and Stella for a while, and she hoped they weren't wearing out their new owner too much. Mrs Hunter was quite old. Molly had helped to bring Star and Stella back together after Mrs Hunter had bought Star, without knowing that she was a magical wish puppy and needed her twin. Molly had been the only person who could tell what was really wrong with Star when she had come into Molly's dad's veterinary surgery. Sometimes being able to talk to magical animals was a big help!

Molly grinned at herself in the mirror. By the time Kitty's birthday party was finished, she was bound to be covered in cake and ice cream, but at least she could start off looking nice!

Kitty was downstairs already, in her new purple birthday dress, with no less than six *I am 4!* badges on. Mum had tried to persuade her not to wear them all, but Kitty was being stubborn, and it *was* her birthday, so she'd got away with it.

"Is he here yet? Is he here yet? When *will* he be here?" Kitty was jumping up and down by the living room window, which looked out on to the lane. "Can you see him, Molly?"

Molly looked out. "No. Who?"

"The Amazing Albert! The magician!" Kitty stared at her as though she were mad. Then she went back to the window. "Oh! Look at that car! That has to be his car!"

A beautiful old red Rolls Royce was purring slowly up the lane, and turning into the yard outside Larkfield Farm, Molly and Kitty's home. Kitty raced back to the kitchen door and out into the yard, watching as the Rolls parked outside their dad's surgery. An elderly man got out, wearing a red tailcoat, with the most enormous white moustache Molly had ever seen. He spotted Molly and Kitty at once, and bowed, very low. Kitty was delighted, and curtseyed back, holding out her purple dress.

Molly's dad came out to help the magician carry in all his boxes, and Kitty's guests started to arrive too. Molly was kept busy showing them where to put their presents, and telling everyone where to go, but she couldn't help peeking out into the back garden every so often. She hadn't been very excited when Mum said there would be a magician, but that was before she saw the Amazing Albert. He just looked – well, magical.

It was a wonderful afternoon, really sunny, even though it was the beginning of October. The magic show was set up in the garden, with all the children sitting round on shiny red cushions that the magician had brought with him. Dad had joked that he must have a magic car, he'd fitted so much stuff into it, but the Amazing Albert had just smiled.

The magician was now wearing a tall, scarlet top hat as well. He looked brilliant, and all Kitty's friends gasped when he made bunches of flowers appear out of nowhere (he gave them to Molly's mum). Then he juggled with flaming torches, and rode on a unicycle. At last, he blew the torches out, and crouched down closer to the children.

"Do you like my hat?" he asked, in a very serious voice, and everyone nodded.

He swept it off his head, and held it out in front of him. "Would you like to see what's inside it?"

"A bunny rabbit!" Kitty gasped excitedly, and the magician laughed.

"Not yet. Look, completely empty. But now..." He put in his hand, and felt around, frowning. "Where's she got to?" Then he poked his nose into the hat, and everyone giggled. "Snowdrop! Where are you? Aha!" And he pulled out a beautiful snow-white rabbit, her fur sparkling in the sunshine. "This is Snowdrop!"

The rabbit stared round at the children, her nose twitching with interest. She was the prettiest rabbit Molly had ever seen, with big dark eyes, and almost silvery-looking fur.

"Now, Kitty, as it's your birthday, Snowdrop and I would like you to help us with this next bit. And perhaps your big sister too," the Amazing Albert added, looking thoughtfully at Molly. "That's it, come on out here. Now, I shall put Snowdrop back..." He laid a red silk handkerchief over the top of the hat, and then whisked it away. "And you can see, everyone, the hat is now empty! Now, Kitty and Molly, see if you can lift her out again."

As soon as Molly reached into the hat with Kitty, and touched Snowdrop's silky fur, she knew that she wasn't just any rabbit. There was a wonderful warm, tingling feeling rushing through her fingers, and the hat seemed to be full of pink sparkles – her fingers were glittering.

And when they pulled Snowdrop out of the hat, she wasn't a white rabbit any more.

She was pink!

Molly gasped, and everyone in the audience *oooh*ed with delight. Snowdrop looked up at Molly, and Molly was *almost* certain she winked. Then she went back to staring innocently out at the audience.

Molly could hardly sit still for the rest of the magic show, she was so excited. Snowdrop simply had to be magical.

Not everyone was as convinced as Molly was, though. Her cousin Louis was sitting at the back next to her, and he just looked bored. He was a couple of years older than Molly, but they got on pretty well.

"Isn't she brilliant?" Molly whispered excitedly.

Louis looked at her disgustedly. "Oh, come on, Molly. You don't believe it's real magic, do you? It's all a trick. It's obvious!

You can't really make a rabbit change colour!"

Molly just stared straight ahead, smiling a little. Maybe not. But a *magic* rabbit could do it all by herself...

At the end of the show, Albert invited everyone to come and stroke Snowdrop. Molly was desperate to go up, but she hung back, hoping that all the others would want to go and start tea, and she might get a moment to talk to Snowdrop without anyone listening.

They were the only ones left in the garden now. Shyly, Molly went up to the Amazing Albert's table, where Snowdrop was sitting while the magician packed away his tricks. Was it her imagination, or was Snowdrop staring at her too?

"Please may I stroke her?" Molly

asked politely, and the magician smiled.
"Of course!" He twirled his moustache,
watching Molly thoughtfully.

Molly put out her hand to stroke
Snowdrop's ears, but the white rabbit
shook her head, and jumped straight into
Molly's arms instead. Molly gasped – she
could really feel Snowdrop's magic now.
A wonderful warmth was running all
the way down to her toes, like she was
drinking sparkly hot chocolate.

"You *are* magic!" Molly whispered happily. "I thought so!"

"Well, you are too!" the rabbit promptly replied. "Didn't I tell you?" she demanded, looking over Molly's shoulder at the magician.

"Yes, yes, I know, she can hear you talking." He was nodding delightedly. "Snowdrop said she thought you were different, when you pulled her out of the hat. And of course, when she came out pink, I knew there was something special about you. Snowdrop doesn't turn pink for many people."

"Can you do other colours too?" Molly asked Snowdrop, impressed.

Snowdrop looked smug. "Of course. Any colour you like!" she boasted. "Even stripes!"

"Only on a good day," Albert reminded

her. "At that party last week you were a very plain brown, *and* you smelled of fish."

Snowdrop sniffed, and twitched her ears as though she didn't like to be reminded. "He was a very unpleasant little boy," she said loftily. "He was picking his nose. Molly is *nice*. Look!" Snowdrop wrinkled her nose, and closed her eyes, and then her tail turned purple.

"Oh, that's fantastic!" Molly giggled.

"So Molly, tell me, have you always been able to talk to animals? Snowdrop's never spoken to anyone but me before, this is a most exciting day for us!" Albert twirled his moustache with one finger, making it curlier than ever. He looked really delighted to have met Molly.

Molly beamed at him. "No, I only realized a few weeks ago. I met a magic

kitten called Sparkle, and then two wish
puppies, Star and Stella. But that's all. I've
never met a magic rabbit. And I only
know one other person who can talk to
animals – Sparkle's owner. She's a witch
who lives in Larkfield Wood."

Albert nodded. "It's a rare gift, and very
special. Oh my goodness!" He checked his

watch. "Snowdrop, we must go! We have another party, Molly. I'm sorry we can't stay, but I'm sure we'll see you again."

Molly helped him carry his boxes to the car and waved them off, then she wandered slowly back to the party, smiling happily to herself.

She'd met a witch's kitten, and two wish puppies, and now a magic rabbit. A rabbit who could change colour, and vanish into a hat. Albert was right – it was a wonderful day!

Chapter Two

The Hiccupping Bunny

Molly wasn't sure how she was going
to see Snowdrop and Albert again. She
wished they hadn't had to dash off so
quickly. Albert had said they would meet
again, but Molly couldn't see how. It
was all a bit disappointing – she'd met a
gorgeous magic bunny, and she'd hardly
had a chance to talk to her! She couldn't
stop thinking about rabbits all week,
and her teacher told her off for drawing
rabbits on her science worksheet.

On Friday afternoon, Molly ran over to the surgery to see if her dad wanted any help. She looked interestedly round the waiting room, and wondered why the man in the brown jacket looked so familiar. He was bending over a box on his lap, but when he looked up, Molly recognized the moustache at once – it was Albert!

"Molly!" He sounded very pleased to see her.

Snowdrop popped her head out of the box at once, her whiskers twitching with delight. "Hello!" she whispered, as Molly crouched down next to her.

"Snowdrop?" Molly's dad was looking round the surgery door. "Oh! Aren't you...?"

"The Amazing Albert, yes." Albert smiled.

"Kitty's still talking about you!" Dad waved them in. "So, what's wrong with Snowdrop? She seemed very healthy at the party. Beautiful condition."

Albert lifted Snowdrop out and cuddled her. "It sounds silly, but – she keeps getting the hiccups. It started a few days ago, soon after Kitty's party, actually. They go on for so long, and I'm just a bit worried about her. She's never had them before."

Molly's dad looked intrigued. "Well, I've never had that one before." He looked at Snowdrop thoughtfully. "No other symptoms, just hiccups? I might have to go and look that up... Would you mind waiting a minute?"

As soon as Molly's dad had gone, Albert gave Molly a worried look. "I couldn't really tell your father, Molly, but it's *not* just hiccups..." He stroked Snowdrop anxiously. "She disappears! Not always, but every so often, she hiccups, and then she vanishes! I don't know what to do!"

Molly looked at Snowdrop, expecting

her to be worried too, but Snowdrop almost looked as though she was smiling. "It's fun," she whispered to Molly.

"Yesterday we did another birthday party, and Snowdrop started hiccupping inside my top hat. I could feel it shaking! And then when she was supposed to disappear, she did, but she didn't come back!" Albert shook his head worriedly. "I had to pretend it was part of the show."

Snowdrop wriggled crossly in his arms. "I did come back, in that special present," she reminded him. "Everyone was very impressed!"

"Yes, but it was in the pass-the-parcel," Albert explained to Molly. "And they were impressed, but that little girl's mother was very confused, Snowdrop. She couldn't work out where the box of crayons had gone. Nor can I, for that matter."

Molly could just imagine what her mum would have said if she'd found a rabbit in Kitty's pass-the-parcel. "And you really don't have any idea why?" she wondered, watching as Snowdrop wriggled out of Albert's arms, and went to explore the rest of the surgery.

"No," Albert sighed. Then he murmured, very quietly, so Snowdrop couldn't hear, "And I can't help worrying, what if next time she doesn't come back?"

Just then Molly's dad came back in, still holding a very large book on rabbits and everything that could possibly go wrong with them.

"I *think* she may just have an upset stomach," he said. "Not too serious. I'll give her some soothing medicine, and you need to keep a careful eye on her diet. No lettuce!"

Albert looked relieved, but then he frowned. "Is there any chance it could be catching?" he asked worriedly.

"Well, it could be a virus, yes. Like stomach flu in humans," Dad agreed.

Albert shook his head. "Oh well. I suppose I'll have to cancel," he said sadly.

"What's wrong?" Molly asked. "Do you have another party?"

"No," Albert sighed. "A big magicians' conference, in Edinburgh. I'd been quite looking forward to it, but it starts tomorrow and I won't be back until Tuesday. I can't risk Snowdrop giving hiccups to all those other rabbits, it just wouldn't be fair."

Snowdrop was scrabbling at his trouser leg, and he picked her up and stroked her ears sadly. She gazed round at them all, her eyes anxious.

"Snowdrop could stay here at the vet's!" Molly suggested excitedly. "We'd look after her for you, then you'd still be able to go."

"Oh, Molly, hang on," Dad said, shaking his head. "Normally I'd say yes, of course we could, but we're really busy this weekend, and Jenny's on holiday, remember? Jenny's our veterinary nurse, Albert. I'm really sorry, I'm just not sure we can fit in looking after Snowdrop too."

"I'll look after her!" Molly said eagerly. She was standing on tiptoe, gazing hopefully up at her dad and Albert.

"I could, honestly. I know loads about rabbits, I really do."

"I'm not sure, Molly. . ." Dad murmured doubtfully.

"I could! Dad, I'm nearly eight, you know! Lots of my friends have pets. I'm not too young, I promise."

"It *is* only for a few days," Albert put in, looking at Molly's dad pleadingly. "I'm sure Molly would look after Snowdrop beautifully. They seemed to get on very well at the party."

"And if Snowdrop's tummy upset got worse, Dad, she'd be in the right place!" Molly pointed out.

Snowdrop wrinkled her nose, and gazed at Molly's dad too.

Molly was almost sure she heard a faint tinkling sound, like little bells, and the air seemed to shimmer pink for a second. She caught her breath. Was Snowdrop doing magic?

Dad shook his head slightly, as though he was feeling dizzy. Then he looked thoughtfully at Molly. "Oh, all right..." he sighed. "But you're going to have to be very responsible, Molly."

Then Snowdrop winked at her. There
was no doubt about it this time. Snowdrop
had magicked her dad into saying yes!

"Wonderful!" Albert cried, hugging
Snowdrop. "I'll bring Snowdrop's hutch
round tomorrow morning before I leave."

"We could put it in the shed, couldn't
we, Dad?" Molly suggested. She really

wanted her dad to see how much she knew about looking after animals. "Rabbits shouldn't be outside all night now it's getting chillier. And we get foxes around here. She'd be much safer in the shed. I can go and tidy it up, Dad! You'll get a tidy shed too!"

"Mmm." Dad still didn't sound convinced, but at least he wasn't saying no.

"Thanks, Dad," Molly said, putting an arm round him. "Honestly, I'll look after Snowdrop so well. You'll see!" Molly just couldn't keep the smile off her face. She went to stroke Snowdrop's nose, and whispered, "You're coming to stay with me!" It was so exciting!

Snowdrop gave her whiskers a delicate little shiver, and they glittered pink for a second. She looked excited too.

Molly sighed happily. At last she was

going to have the chance to show Mum and Dad how well she could look after a pet. It was almost as if her special wish puppy wish for a pet of her own was starting to come true!

Chapter Three

Snowdrop Settles In

Molly got up super-early on Saturday morning to tidy the shed ready for Snowdrop's hutch. It wasn't much of a fun job. The shed was full of gardening tools, and seed packets, and spiders. Kitty kept trying to help, and then shrieking and running away whenever she saw even a leg of a spider. But it was worth it to have a pet, even if Snowdrop was borrowed, and only Molly's for three days.

Snowdrop's hutch was huge. It almost

filled the back seat of Albert's car, and Dad had to help him carry it in. They set it up in the shed, and then Albert took Snowdrop out to say goodbye.

"Be good!" he told her firmly. "Don't be naughty for Molly. And *please* try not to hiccup!" he added in a whisper. Then he handed her to Molly, and looked worriedly at them both. "I do hope you'll be all right," he murmured. "I've never left her with anyone else before."

"You'll be late if you don't set off soon," Snowdrop told him. "Molly and I will be fine. Won't we?" There were pink sparkles fizzing round her ears, and she had a look of mischief in her eyes.

Molly nodded happily. "We really will!" she promised. She hadn't noticed Snowdrop's mischievous glance.

Albert handed her an enormous bag

of carrots. "Her favourite..." he muttered. Then he rushed off to his car, without looking back.

Snowdrop was Molly's now!

It was wonderful, having a pet, especially one who could talk back! Molly spent most of the day in the garden with Snowdrop, chatting, although of course they had to be careful when Mum or Dad or Kitty were around. Snowdrop was very funny. Molly soon discovered that she liked to have things her own way, and she was quite fussy. She liked eating daisies, but only the yellow middles, and she insisted that Molly had to pick the petals off one by one, as they tasted better that way. Molly tried pulling all the petals off at once when she wasn't looking, but Snowdrop spat that one out, and gave her a reproachful look.

"Sorry..." Molly said, trying not to laugh. Snowdrop's face was so funny. After that, she didn't try to argue when Snowdrop demanded that her stomach medicine had to be fed to her drop by drop on wafer-thin slices of peeled carrot. It was easier just to do as she was told.

"Molly! Teatime!"

Molly jumped up. "Oh, that's Mum. I'll

pop you back in your hutch, but don't worry, I'll come back out to see you after tea."

Snowdrop nodded, and hopped back into her sleeping quarters. Molly was sure that the hutch was actually bigger on the inside, as it seemed to have at least four rooms. "I shall have a rest," Snowdrop said grandly. "This has been rather a tiring day." She lay down on her back in the

hay, with her paws in the air, and closed
her eyes. "You could bring me some
grated carrot later, perhaps," she suggested.
"As a little bedtime something..."

After tea, Dad came back out with Molly
to check that Snowdrop was settling
down well in her new home. Molly
grinned to herself when Dad said this.
Sometimes she wished she could tell him
that some of the animals spoke to her.
But she didn't think he would believe
her – he would say she'd imagined it.
Right now it would be fun to be able to
say that Snowdrop was fine – but she'd
asked for grated carrot for supper, and
she didn't approve of the view from her
hutch, because the lawnmower was too
grubby. Molly had promised to wipe it.

"I wonder if that medicine's working

yet?" Dad said thoughtfully to Molly as they walked down the garden. "Have you noticed Snowdrop hiccupping at all today?"

"No." Molly shook her head. "Maybe she's better. It would be great to be able to tell Albert we'd cured her, wouldn't it?" Molly skipped ahead excitedly as Dad stopped to see how his flowerbeds were looking. She would love to be able to welcome Albert back on Tuesday with the news that Snowdrop was all better.

But just as she opened the shed door – it was sticking a bit, so it took a minute – Molly heard a hiccup. Not very loud, but definitely a *hic!* She sighed. Oh dear... There was another one, and another, and then a flash of golden light lit up the hutch. Molly caught one glimpse of Snowdrop's startled face, peeping out of the wire front of the hutch, and then there was a loud *pop!* and she disappeared.

Then Dad walked into the shed – to find Snowdrop gone.

Molly was peering into the back of the hutch, trying to work out if Snowdrop was still there, just invisible, or if she'd actually *gone* somewhere.

"Molly, what are you doing?" Dad

asked, sounding surprised. "Snowdrop's not going to like you sticking your head in her hutch like that! Can you get her out for me, so I can check her over?"

Molly closed her eyes tightly, then opened them again and looked back in the hutch, hoping that Snowdrop would have miraculously reappeared. But she hadn't.

"No."

Dad blinked. "What?"

"I can't get her out ... she, umm ... she isn't here, Dad..." Molly twisted her fingers worriedly. What else could she say?

"But – but where is she? Molly! You can't have lost her, we've only had her for a day? What happened?" Dad sounded really cross. "Did you leave the hutch open?"

"No! Of course not!" Molly said, her

voice hurt. She was far too sensible to do that!

"Molly, you must have done, how else could she have got out? I knew this was a bad idea." Dad shook his head. "Right, you search in here, see if she's hiding behind any of the gardening things, and I'll go and look outside. I just hope she hasn't got out of the garden, we might never find her." Dad rushed out on to the lawn, and Molly followed him, trying to explain, but what could she say? Dad wasn't going to believe that Snowdrop had vanished all by herself.

Molly walked back into the shed, and stared anxiously into Snowdrop's hutch. "Snowdrop! Snowdrop!" she whispered. "Please come back! I'm really worried about you, and Dad's so cross, he thinks I let you out. Please come back as soon as you can!"

Nothing happened. Molly could hear Dad calling crossly in the garden and running up and down, searching under the bushes.

"Please, Snowdrop!" she whispered again.

All at once there was another flash of golden light, and Snowdrop was back. She was sitting on top of her hutch now, looking slightly dazed. "*Hic!*" she said loudly. And then, "Hello, Molly!"

"Sssshhh! My dad's here, he's looking
for you. He thinks you're lost. Please will
you get back in your hutch, he's so cross!"

Snowdrop sighed, and let Molly slip
her back into the hutch, just as Dad came
striding back into the shed. "There's no sign,
Molly. This is why Mum and I were worried
about you having a pet. You have to be so
careful — hey, where did she come from?"

"She was there all the time, Dad!" Molly said, trying to smile, and shutting the hutch door *very* tightly. "I think she was hidden behind her hay bed, I just couldn't see her!" She felt a bit guilty, because it wasn't strictly true. But after all, she hadn't left the door open, and Snowdrop hadn't *really* gone out of the shed, had she?

"But I looked too..." Dad muttered.

"She just wasn't there. You are one tricksy bunny," he told Snowdrop sternly. "I'm getting a bad feeling about this weekend." He sighed. "Don't be long, Molly, all right? And make sure you close that hutch up tightly! I don't trust that rabbit, at all. . ."

Chapter Four

Snowdrop at School

Molly tried to get Snowdrop to explain where she'd been, so she'd be able to find her if it happened again, but Snowdrop said she didn't know.

"It was somewhere sparkly," she said, not very helpfully. "And it smelled nice."

It wasn't a lot to go on.

Molly just had to hope that Snowdrop wouldn't get hiccups when Dad was around. She didn't think he'd believe the story about losing Snowdrop in the hay *again*.

"I wish I knew how to cure you," she told Snowdrop on Sunday afternoon. They were sitting in the shed doorway, Snowdrop on Molly's lap, her eyes blissfully closed as Molly stroked her ears over and over.

"Mmm."

Molly got the feeling Snowdrop wasn't really listening.

"Mum tells me to hold my breath and

count to ten when I get hiccups, have you tried that?"

"Rabbits aren't good at holding their breath," Snowdrop said, stretching her front paws out lazily, so that she was flopped all across Molly's lap.

"When I got hiccups at Grandad's house once, he gave me a spoonful of sugar to stop them, but I don't think sugar's good for rabbits..." Molly sighed.

Snowdrop's ears twitched with interest. "Perhaps we should try..." she said hopefully.

Molly giggled. "Snowdrop, you are so greedy!"

"I only want to cure my hiccups," Snowdrop protested, trying to look innocent.

Molly tickled her ears. "I'll miss you when I'm at school tomorrow," she said sadly.

Snowdrop sat up at once. "School? You mean you won't be here?"

"Well, no, tomorrow's Monday! I have to go to school, Snowdrop, even though you're here. I'm really sorry. You don't get days off because of rabbits."

"Well, you should..." Snowdrop muttered grumpily. "I don't like being on my own, it's very boring. I wanted to go to the conference, and I wasn't allowed, and now you're leaving me too!"

Snowdrop sulked on and off for the rest of the day, until Molly brought her a whole bowl of grated carrot before she went to bed. Then she let Molly kiss her nose, and even said sorry for being so bad-tempered.

But the next morning Snowdrop had had an idea. "Can't I come to school too?" she asked hopefully.

"No!" Molly said, sounding horrified. "We aren't allowed pets at school, ever! I mean, we do have a school guinea pig, but we can't bring our own pets into school. I'm sorry, Snowdrop. I just came to fill up your food and water bowls. And I brought you some beautiful carrots, see..."

Snowdrop sniffed. But then her eyes brightened, and she picked up one of the carrots in her teeth. As Molly took out the bowls to refill them, Snowdrop hopped up on top of the hutch, where Molly had left her lunch box. Snowdrop wasn't just any rabbit after all. She had learned lots of useful tricks with Albert, and she was quite capable of opening a lunch box, without even using magic. She quickly dropped the carrot inside, and glanced back down at Molly, who

was still making sure there were lots of
sunflower seeds in her food bowl.

"Albert said you really liked them, so
I'm giving you some extra ones, OK?"

Snowdrop blew a waft of glittery,
golden breath on the carrot that made it
go all sparkly.

She twitched her nose in a satisfied
sort of way, and nudged the lunch box
shut. Done. "That's hardly any!" Snowdrop

protested, peering down at her food bowl. "Lots more than that!"

Molly shook a few more in. "There you go! You've got loads now. Have a nice day, and I'll be back by afternoon snack time! See you later!"

"Goodbye, Molly!" Snowdrop watched her carefully shutting the hutch door. She was planning to see Molly a little sooner than Molly thought...

Rabbits seemed to keep popping up at school that morning. The maths problems were about how long it would take how many rabbits to eat a field of lettuces, and two of Molly's friends had new rabbit pencil cases. It made Molly jittery. She really hoped Snowdrop was behaving herself!

At lunch time, Molly sat and stared at her lunch box. She didn't really feel hungry. But she could feel one of the teachers watching her, so she opened it up at last.

There was a carrot inside.

A whole carrot, with the green feathery leaves still on the top. Molly blinked at it. Mum sometimes gave her carrot sticks in a little pot, but not a whole one! It looked awfully like one of the carrots she'd given Snowdrop that morning...

As she stared, the carrot started to sparkle – just little golden glimmers round the leaves. Molly gulped, and grabbed it, hiding it in her lap. Luckily all her friends were complaining about the test Miss Fraser had given them that morning (which Molly couldn't even remember) and hadn't noticed. Molly quickly took off her cardigan, and put it over the carrot. She had a horrible feeling she knew what was about to happen.

She was right. There was a funny little noise, rather like a hiccup, and a flash of golden light, which luckily was mostly hidden under Molly's cardigan. Then the cardigan wriggled, and Snowdrop's silvery-white nose peeped out.

"Hello Molly!" she squeaked excitedly. "I've come to school too!"

"How did you get here?" Molly whispered, tucking Snowdrop's ears back under her cardigan. "We mustn't let anyone see you!"

"I put a finding spell on the carrot, so I could follow it when I hiccupped. It was very clever of me. Aren't you impressed?" Snowdrop sounded smug.

"Of course I am, but we're going to get into trouble. I told you, we aren't allowed pets!" Molly looked round anxiously, but no one seemed to have spotted that she was talking to her cardigan.

Snowdrop wasn't listening. "I'm soooo hungry! It was hard work, that spell," she moaned.

"Eat the carrot!" Molly said crossly.

"I'm bored with carrots now. I'd like something else. Maybe some lettuce. Have you got any?" Snowdrop started to creep out from under the cardigan, and Molly grabbed her in horror.

"No!"

"OW!" Snowdrop squeaked loudly, and everyone looked at Molly. Molly looked behind her, trying to pretend she didn't know what the noise was either. Then there was another *pop!* and a flash, and Snowdrop wasn't huddled under Molly's cardigan any more.

So where was she?

Knowing Snowdrop, Molly thought, she would be looking for food. She'd wanted lettuce. Molly looked round to see if anyone had lettuce in their sandwiches. She had to get Snowdrop back before

someone spotted her... Then she noticed
a spot of white over by the dinner
queue – Snowdrop had found the salad
bar! She was sitting happily on the edge
of a big metal tray of lettuce, nibbling
away blissfully.

Molly stood up, wondering how on
earth she was going to get Snowdrop

out of there without anyone seeing her. But she was too late. There was a sudden scream, and one of the dinner ladies threw a ladle at Snowdrop. "It's a rat!" she yelled, then she fainted with horror, collapsing in a heap behind the counter.

Snowdrop jumped into the air in panic, then there was an enormous *pop!* and she disappeared completely, leaving everyone wondering just what was going on.

Molly ran across the room, hunting for Snowdrop, but she couldn't see her anywhere. It didn't help that half the girls in the school (and some of the boys) thought Snowdrop had been a rat too, and were standing on their chairs screaming.

Molly spent the whole of lunch time searching, but Snowdrop was nowhere to be seen. She'd got such a fright,

Molly just didn't know where she might have gone. She was really hoping that Snowdrop had jumped back to her hutch, where she would feel safe. But when Molly finally got back from school, and raced down the garden to the shed, there was no welcoming squeak from Snowdrop's hutch. It was quite empty.

Molly sat down on the step, blinking away tears. Crying wouldn't help. Snowdrop was gone – and Molly had no idea how to get her back.

Chapter Five

The Sparkly Spell

Molly sat staring out into the garden, desperately trying to think of places Snowdrop might be. She couldn't give up! She just hoped that Snowdrop wasn't frightened, or hurt.

There was a rustling in the bushes, and Molly looked up sharply. It was only a blackbird, but Molly got up to search round the garden anyway. Snowdrop didn't seem to have an awful lot of control when she disappeared without expecting to. Maybe she'd aimed for her hutch and missed?

She was just peering under the wheelbarrow that Dad had left out, when Kitty came up beside her, very quietly. "What are you doing?" she asked, and Molly jumped and banged her head on the wheelbarrow.

"Nothing!" she snapped crossly. But it was lucky that it had been Kitty who caught her, not Mum or Dad. She mustn't let them find out that Snowdrop had disappeared! She had to find her first!

But as Molly realized this, Dad came walking down the garden. "Mum wants you, Kitty. Hi Molly, how was school? Have you been to see Snowdrop? Did she miss you today?"

"Mmm!" Molly didn't know quite what to say. She cast an anxious glance down to the shed, at the bottom of the garden.

"I'll just have a quick look at her before tea." Dad carried on down the path.

"Oh, no, she's all right!" Molly gasped out.

"It's OK, Molly, I'm sure she's fine – you've done so well looking after her." Dad put an arm round Molly's shoulders. "I have to say, Molly, I'm really impressed.

You've been very responsible."

Molly felt sick – she'd been hoping that Dad would say something like this, and she'd been waiting for her parents to notice how well she was looking after Snowdrop, but why did it have to be *now*? When Dad was just about to find out that Snowdrop was gone. Molly suddenly knew that she couldn't – mustn't – let Dad see the empty hutch.

But what was she going to do? Suddenly the magical locket that Sparkle the kitten had given her seemed to grow warm around her neck under her school shirt. Molly put her hand up to it. It felt glittery and buzzy and special, and Molly took a deep breath. It was like a magical message from Sparkle, telling her she had to do a spell – but Molly had never done magic on her own before.

Dad had let go of her and was strolling on, muttering to himself about needing to cut the grass, it was full of daisies. He was right.

The daisies made Molly think of Snowdrop, and her fussy daisy-eating. Her eyes pricked with tears. Molly knelt down and picked a handful of daisies, hurriedly pulling off the petals one by one.

Dad was almost at the shed now.

Molly closed her eyes and threw the handful of daisy petals up in the air, whispering, *Stop him!* to herself. They seemed to hang in the late afternoon light for a few seconds, fluttering and shimmering silver. Then they floated down, and some of them landed in Molly's dad's hair. He stopped, and ran one hand across his face, looking confused.

"Oh, Molly, now what was I meant to be doing? It's always the same, you get down to the end of the garden and forget what you went for." He sighed, and wandered slowly back to the house.

Molly stared after him, with her mouth hanging open. That was the first time she had done magic all by herself – and it had worked! A thrill of delight ran through her – she felt so proud!

But there was no time to celebrate, she still had a missing bunny to find...

Worn out from searching all afternoon, Molly cried herself to sleep that night. She couldn't help imagining Snowdrop, lost and alone somewhere, probably frightened, with no idea how to get home. Albert was coming home tomorrow, and he would be really looking forward to seeing her. How could Molly tell him Snowdrop was lost?

But in the middle of the night, Molly woke up with a jump. She'd been dreaming of carrots. Feathery-leaved, orange and green and silver-sparkly carrots. Just like the one that Snowdrop had used in her naughty spell to appear at school. Molly sat up in bed, staring into the darkness, her breathing fast and trembly with excitement. The carrot – she still had the carrot! It was in her school bag, wasn't it?

Molly slid out of bed, tiptoed across her floor, and made for the stairs as fast as she could. She crept down them in the darkness, feeling her way by hugging the banister. There was a little moonlight shining through the glass in the front door, so she could almost see. Her school bag was sitting in the hallway, and Molly ferreted through it. There was something round, and cold – no, that was a water bottle... But here it was! She could feel the cool, feathery leaves, and the tingle of magic as her fingers closed round it. Molly dashed back up the stairs, and curled up back in her bed, holding the carrot in shivery hands.

"Snowdrop! Snowdrop!" she whispered. "Where are you? Find your way back!"

There was a flash of golden, glittering light, like there had been at school, and Molly caught her breath excitedly, sure that Snowdrop would come bouncing on to her bed.

But she didn't. No bunny hiccupped, and the carrot was just a carrot again.

Chapter Six

A Cure For Hiccups

Molly woke to hear Mum calling her from the doorway.

"Molly! Molly! Wake up! You haven't overslept, have you? You must have had a busy day at school yesterday. Get dressed and come down quickly, Molly, Albert's here! He drove all night to get back and see Snowdrop, he was missing her so much."

Molly blinked sleepily. Albert. Snowdrop. It took a few seconds for the names to mean anything, then it all flooded back.

Albert was here to fetch Snowdrop, and Molly didn't have her!

The spell hadn't worked, and Molly had fallen asleep again eventually, still clutching the carrot. She felt awful. She could hear Albert's voice downstairs, talking to Mum and Dad. He sounded happy and excited, as though he'd had a great time at the conference. There was an eager tone to his voice as well. Obviously he was waiting for Molly to come down and take him to see Snowdrop. It was nice of him to wait.

Molly sniffed, burying her nose in her pillow. She didn't want to get up and tell everyone the truth. Oh, why hadn't it worked? The carrot was on the pillow next to her, the long green leaves tickling her chin.

And giggling. Molly opened her eyes, slowly. She was fairly sure that even

carrots with spells on them didn't giggle.
But magical rabbits did, and their whiskers
were tickly and tingly...

"Oh, do wake up!" a soft little voice
muttered in her ear. "Come on, Molly,
haven't you missed me?"

It *had* worked! Molly sat straight
upright, almost knocking Snowdrop off
her pillow. "Where *were* you?" she gasped.

Snowdrop shuddered. "I don't know! It was horrible, it was *very* far away, and it was all dark. I didn't like it at all. I was so happy when I heard you calling me. It took a while to get back, that was all. I'd been trying to look for Albert, but it was hard when I'd never been to that Edinburgh place."

"Ohhh!" Molly breathed, hugging Snowdrop delightedly. "I thought it hadn't worked! I was so worried about you!"

Snowdrop nudged Molly's chin with her nose, in a sorry sort of way. "I shouldn't have followed you to school, Molly, it was my own fault I got lost in that dark place, and you saved me. Albert will be very grateful."

Molly jumped out of bed. "Did you hear? Mum said he's downstairs. I need to get dressed and get down there."

"And you need to get me back into my hutch!" Snowdrop pointed out. "Albert wouldn't mind me being up here, but I don't think your mum would like it. Can I take the carrot? I'm starving!"

Molly was pulling on her school uniform. "Can't you magic yourself back?" she asked, halfway inside her shirt.

Snowdrop was silent for a minute. Then, "I don't think so," she said doubtfully. "I think something's happened... I'm sure I can disappear with you or Albert to help me, but I don't think I can do it on my own any more. The hiccup feeling's gone, and that's what was making me jumpy..."

"You're not hiccupping any more? Really?" Molly picked Snowdrop up and stared at her thoughtfully. "But that's amazing! You're cured! I wonder how, though?"

Snowdrop gave a little shiver. "Well, I don't *know*, but I think that horrible woman throwing something at me had something to do with it. Every time I want to hiccup, I can't help thinking of her! Uugggh!"

Molly laughed. "Of course, a fright! That's the best cure for hiccups there is! It's what Dad always tries to do when me or Kitty have them, only he's useless at it and he just makes us laugh. I can't believe we solved the problem without even trying!"

Snowdrop nodded. "It's a pity, I shall miss those funny magic jumps. But Albert will be relieved. Please, Molly, I do want to see him so much. If you hold me, and we both think of my hutch, I'm sure I can get there. Then you can go down and fetch him for me."

"OK." Molly held Snowdrop tightly, and thought of the pretty, blue-painted hutch, the sweet-smelling hay bed, Snowdrop's food bowls...

There was a twinkling fizz of golden light, and Snowdrop disappeared from her arms. Molly looked at the suddenly empty space, and giggled. She'd just done another spell! But now she had to get downstairs to see Albert! She flung open her bedroom door, and raced to the stairs.

"She looks wonderful!" Albert said admiringly, stroking Snowdrop's tummy as she lay on her back in his arms.

Molly looked round to check that Mum and Dad weren't listening. "And we cured the hiccups!" she whispered. "Snowdrop will tell you – she got a bit of a fright, and now she can't hiccup-jump any more!"

"Oh, Snowdrop, were you doing something you shouldn't? I told you to be good for Molly," Albert sighed.

"I was only a little naughty," Snowdrop yawned. "Molly is very nice, but I did miss you. You know how to peel carrots exactly right." She rubbed her ears against his sleeve lovingly.

Molly grinned at Albert. She had loved having Snowdrop as a borrowed pet, but she *was* bossy!

"Molly did well, don't you think, Albert?" Molly's dad asked, as he came out of the shed, lugging Snowdrop's hutch.

"Oh, very well. Better than you can imagine!" Albert said, smiling.

"Like I said before, Molly, I'm really proud of you." Dad glanced at Mum, and she nodded. "You know, we think you're almost ready for a pet of your own."

Molly beamed at them both, and then caught Snowdrop's eye. The silver-white rabbit's fur twinkled pink for just a second, and she winked.

Molly winked back. She was so

happy — she'd wished for a pet when Star
and Stella gave her a wish, and now it
was starting to come true. And she'd done
magic, all by herself! That was almost
as exciting. Perhaps she'd be able to use
her spells to help another magical animal
soon. . .

The Secret Pony

Chapter One

My Own Pony

Molly wandered down the lane, humming to herself, and enjoying the bright autumn sunshine. She stopped halfway along to climb on the gate that led to the riding school fields. Lots of the ponies were turned out there this morning. Molly had hoped they would be, and she'd raided her mum's cupboard for sugar lumps.

Molly stood on the bottom rung of the gate, which made her just the right height to lean over the top and call to

the ponies, who were already looking up
at her with interest. As soon as Molly
held out her hand with a couple of sugar
lumps, the two nearest ponies trotted
over eagerly. She had ridden at the riding
school a few times, and had often gone
there with her dad, because he was their
vet, so she knew these two ponies. The
chestnut was called Bella, and the black
pony was Treacle.

Molly stroked their noses, and fed them more sugar, and crooned compliments to them, but they didn't talk back. Of course, she didn't really expect them to, but Molly knew that some animals *could* talk, and she had met several who did. Sparkle the witch's kitten, Star and Stella the wish puppies, and just a week or so ago, Snowdrop, the cheeky vanishing rabbit.

When they'd finished up all the sugar, the ponies licked at her hands, and sniffed her pockets hopefully, just in case she had some more sugar or even mints hidden away, then trotted off to graze again.

Molly slid down from the gate, and walked on, thinking about ponies. She had looked after Snowdrop the rabbit for her owner, a magician called the Amazing Albert, while he was away. It had been a tricky job, because Snowdrop was extremely fussy, and she kept accidentally disappearing. But Molly's mum and dad had been really impressed with the way she'd looked after Snowdrop, and they'd said that very soon they'd think about letting Molly have a pet of her own.

Ever since then, Molly had been wondering about what sort of pet she should have. She hadn't really thought about a pony, but she did love to ride. She was quite good at it, and there was plenty of space round the old farmhouse where they lived. A pony of her very own! That would be wonderful. A couple of girls in her class at school had their own ponies, and Jess actually rode to school on hers. She lived a little way out of Larkfield, so she rode in and stabled her pony in a field near to the school.

Molly looked
at her watch
and speeded
up a bit. She'd
spent longer than
she'd realized
talking to Bella
and Treacle.
Grandad would
be expecting her
already. Molly
was heading for
the forge, where her grandad worked
as a blacksmith. It was only half a mile
down the lane from Larkfield Farm Vets,
so she was allowed to walk there on her
own sometimes. But if she was late, and
Grandad got worried and phoned Mum,
there would be a huge fuss.

Besides, she wanted to get to the forge.

Grandad had two horses booked in for shoeing today, and he'd asked Molly to come and help. Even before she had discovered her magical ability, Molly had always been very good at calming nervous animals, and Grandad liked her to hold the horses sometimes.

Usually on a Saturday, Molly would be helping her dad at the surgery, doing the same sort of thing, but Dad was busy with an urgent operation today. He'd even cancelled morning surgery, because a cat had been brought in late last night with very serious injuries after a car accident. This morning Dad was going to operate on the poor cat's leg. Molly nibbled her bottom lip. Dad was worried about the cat, she could tell. Molly had heard him telling Mum that he thought it might be too weak for the operation.

Molly sighed, hoping it was going all right back at the surgery, and ran the last little way down the lane to the forge. A very smart navy blue horsebox was standing outside, and Molly hurried in. The forge was round the back of Grandad's cottage, and a path led up into the yard. There was no sound of hammering, so Grandad hadn't started yet.

Suddenly there was a shrill whinny of fear, a noise that sent a shiver running through Molly's bones. What was going on? Molly had never heard a horse sound that scared, especially not anywhere near Grandad. He was known throughout the whole area as a good blacksmith. He was so gentle with the horses – Molly's mum said that Molly had inherited some of his gift.

She crept into the yard, not wanting to scare the horse any more, and peered over into the open forge.

Then she gasped. Standing in the dim forge, lit by the dancing gas flames, was the most beautiful pony she had ever seen.

Chapter Two

The Silver Pony

The silver-white pony was stamping and struggling and pulling at his lead-rope, obviously very scared. His long, white mane was tossing everywhere, and his big eyes were panicked.

"Oh, Molly!" Grandad sounded glad to see her. "Would you be able to help Mrs James hold Silver? He's a bit nervous."

Mrs James was a tall woman, with very dark hair, and a stern face. She looked at Molly's grandad in surprise, and seemed quite annoyed. "I really don't think a little girl is going to make much difference," she snapped.

Molly stared at her. She was so rude! And it wasn't as if she was managing the pony very well herself. The poor thing was terrified.

Grandad frowned. "Molly is very good at calming horses," he said, his voice polite, but firm.

Just then, the pony took advantage of them all being distracted, and tossed his head high, yanking the lead-rope out of Mrs James's hand.

Then he wheeled round, and backed up against the wall, putting his head down and pawing the ground, as though he was planning to shove his way through them and make a dash out of the forge.

Molly gasped, but not because she was frightened. As the pony ducked his head, just for a second in the firelight, Molly had seen a shining, pearly horn between his ears.

Silver wasn't a pony.

He was a unicorn!

"Horrible animal," Mrs James said angrily. "I don't know what's the matter with him."

Molly didn't dare say it, of course, but she had a feeling that belonging to Mrs James might be quite a lot of what was wrong with Silver. She would upset anyone.

Molly tried hard to remember everything she'd ever read about unicorns, but all she could think of was that their horns were very sharp, which wasn't helpful. Slowly, she took a step towards Silver, who was still pressed back against the wall of the forge, his sides heaving.

He eyed her uncertainly, twisting his head from side to side to see her better, and Molly saw the horn again. She definitely hadn't imagined it. She held out her hand, and gently stroked the side of his neck. He was trembling.

Silver drew a deep, shuddering breath, and nuzzled against Molly's shoulder. He stared into her eyes, and Molly noticed that his own eyes were blue. She had seen a blue-eyed pony once before, but Silver's eyes were a deep, dark blue, like the sea on a summer day. They were beautiful.

You know what I am. . . A soft, gentle voice spoke in her mind, and Molly nodded slightly. She had been wondering if he would talk to her.

"Well, lead him back over here, girl!" Mrs James snapped, and Silver flinched at her voice.

Molly turned and glared at Mrs James. She just stopped herself from being rude back – she didn't want Mrs James to be upset with Grandad. "In a minute," she said, forcing herself to be polite. "He's still very frightened."

I'm not!

I know, but I have to tell her something, Molly explained. It was very odd, talking without saying anything. She'd never been able to do it before, although she had heard Sparkle and Star's voices in her head. *Has she owned you for long?*

She doesn't own me. No one owns me. I was stolen from my home, and I need to find my way back. She wants to put shoes on me, Molly, and I can't let her! Iron shoes will make me just an ordinary pony, I won't be a unicorn any more. You have to help me. . .

I will, Molly promised. She turned back to Grandad and Mrs James. "I can get him to stand, but he won't let you shoe him," she told Grandad.

"What?" Mrs James sounded furious. "What nonsense! He told you that, did he?"

Molly wondered what Mrs James would say if she told her that yes, he had. But it probably wasn't a good idea. "He seems afraid of being shod," she said slowly. It was almost the truth.

"Well, he's never been shod before," Grandad said thoughtfully.

Mrs James stared at him. "Never been shod? Of course he has!"

"I promise you, he hasn't." Grandad came over to Molly and Silver, and gently stroked Silver's nose. Then he carefully lifted up one of Silver's hind feet.

"Look – no nail marks. He's never had shoes."

Mrs James was frowning angrily. "He was sold to me as a gentle riding pony, an ideal beginner's pony for my daughter!"

"Well, I'm afraid he certainly isn't that," Grandad said, looking at Silver's wild eyes, and his hoof that was nervously pawing the dusty stone floor.

"I shall demand my money back," Mrs James muttered.

"Why don't you try taking him to a specialist trainer?" Grandad suggested. "I can give you some people to call. I don't think he's been properly broken for riding, and he may have been mistreated, to be this scared."

"So you're not going to shoe him?" Mrs James demanded, her hands angrily on her hips.

Grandad stared back silently, and Mrs James shifted uncomfortably as he looked at her. "No, I'm not," he finally told her. "This pony is terrified, and I'm not going to risk damaging his spirit for ever. Until he's willing to be shod, I won't shoe him."

I like your grandfather... Silver told Molly.

Me too! Molly replied. She was very impressed with Grandad, especially as Mrs James would probably go and tell all her horsy friends mean things about him.

Mrs James took hold of Silver's lead-rope, and yanked him towards her, dragging him out of the forge.

Molly gasped, and made a move to stop her, but Silver shook his mane, the long silvery-white locks shaking sparkles all over the forge. *Don't worry. She won't keep me for long. I'll be back to find you, Molly. You will help me get home, won't you?*

Molly nodded fiercely. "I promise!" she whispered. She wanted to say it out loud. She looked up as Silver paced out of sight down the little lane to the horse-box, and found Grandad staring at her, puzzled.

"You know, Molly, I've the strangest
feeling that that was no ordinary horse..."

Chapter Three

A Magical Morning

Molly dreamed of unicorns that night, and the next. They were galloping through forests, and leaping over rivers, their hooves leaving silvery trails in the darkness. Then she woke up on Monday morning convinced that someone was calling her. It wasn't properly light in her bedroom yet though. Was Mum really calling her this early? Molly rolled over and looked sleepily at her clock. Five o'clock in the morning! She must have imagined it. Just a dream, probably, she thought, and snuggled back into her duvet.

Molly!

Molly sat up. She definitely hadn't imagined *that*. She threw back her covers, and crept out of bed, shivering a little in the chilly autumn morning. She peeped out through her bedroom curtains, remembering

Sparkle climbing up to her windowsill a few weeks ago, but no one was there.

The orchard, Molly!

Oh! Molly was starting to wake up properly now, and she recognized the voice in her mind. It was Silver, the unicorn – he'd found her at last. She had been worrying that he wouldn't know where she lived. Quickly she threw on her school uniform. That way she wouldn't have to get changed later, and if anyone asked why she was outside, she could just say that she'd woken up early and felt like a walk, although she wasn't sure how convinced Mum would be by that.

Then she tiptoed through the grey, early-morning house, grabbing her jacket and wellies and heading out to the orchard. It was a beautiful morning, cold, but with bright sunshine just starting to break through the swirls of mysterious mist.

Molly leaned on the orchard gate. It was such a magical time of day, with the mist trailing round the trees, and dewdrops on all the hedges. The spiders' webs had turned into diamond necklaces on the bushes by the gate.

It was the perfect morning for a magical adventure, Molly thought to herself, as she blew on her fingers. It would be nice if it warmed up a bit, that was all.

Walking slowly through the mist towards her came a beautiful silver-white creature. It was Silver. His horn was much clearer now – perhaps he could hide it, Molly wondered, if he needed to be in disguise. Maybe she'd only seen it on Saturday because he was upset. It was obvious that Silver wanted her to see it now.

"Hello, Molly," Silver said, out loud this time. His voice was low and musical.

"You came!" Molly said shyly. Silver was so beautiful, she was a little scared to talk to him.

Silver nodded. "When you put your

hand on me, back at the forge, I knew I could trust you. So last night, when the people didn't shut the door of my stable properly, I slipped out after dark, and came to find you. I need your help."

Molly nodded. "I'll try my best. You *are* a unicorn, aren't you? I can hardly believe you're real."

Silver laughed. "I am real. Touch me!" And he stepped closer, nuzzling against Molly's hand.

Molly gently stroked his neck. Such a delicious feeling of warmth ran through her, it sparkled all the way to her fingertips.

"See? You're not imagining me." Silver tossed his mane.

"I've only ever heard of unicorns in fairy tales. Are they everywhere, and I just didn't realize?" Molly was thinking of Bella and Treacle. Were they really unicorns in disguise too?

"No, we're very rare. People hardly ever see us now, it's too dangerous. I live in a hidden wood, deep in the mountains. There's a unicorn herd there – a blessing of unicorns, it's called, when there are lots of us – but I wanted to explore. I went wandering, and I was caught. Oh, they didn't know what I was, they just thought I was a pretty pony, with no owner around, and that they'd sell me on."

"Couldn't you stop them?" Molly asked. Silver's horn looked rather sharp. She would have thought he could fight off anyone who tried to steal him.

Silver sighed. "I was too surprised. And – and I suppose a little bit scared. And I didn't want them to see I was a unicorn. Then they put a metal bridle on me. I can't stand iron, it dulls my powers. That's why I couldn't let your grandfather shoe me, with those iron horseshoes."

"So what happened then?" Molly asked breathlessly.

"They sold me to that woman, Mrs James. She wanted me for her daughter to ride. Alice is a nice girl, a lot nicer than her mother. She seems lonely, they've only been living here a little while, I think, and she doesn't have many friends yet." Silver's eyes were troubled, as though he was worried about the girl.

"Alice! Oh, does she have curly hair? We've got a new girl in our class, she's called Alice."

Silver nodded. "Yes, dark hair, very curly. She's very kind, and brings me apples, and sugar, but she doesn't want to ride me. I think she must have had a fall once, she's scared to ride now, and her mother gets very cross with her about it. I think I was rather expensive..." He snorted, as though he thought this was quite silly. "She likes stroking me though, and she buys me packets of something called Polos. She shares them with me." He sighed. "Delicious..."

Molly looked at him worriedly. "Alice doesn't talk that much at school. She's only been here a couple of weeks, but she's ever so quiet. I've said hello to her a few times, and chatted with her a bit, and she seems really friendly, but she doesn't say much. I think she's still getting used to us. I just wish ... well, I wish you'd belonged to somebody who wasn't so nice."

Silver shook his mane again, showering Molly with silvery sparkles. "I know. She'll be sad that I've gone."

His voice was very quiet. "And I will miss her, even though they kept me shut up, which was horrible." His eyelids fluttered closed for a second, and when they opened again, his eyes were black with fear. "I can't stay there, Molly. If I stay, they'll put those iron shoes on me, and I'll be a prisoner and I'll lose my magic. I have to be free!"

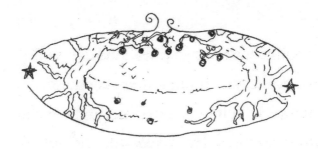

Chapter Four

The Spell in the Orchard

"Can you do magic as well, then?" Molly asked in surprise. Silver was so rare and special, and he could talk in her head, so she hadn't really expected that he could do other magic too.

Silver nodded. "All unicorns have magical powers, Molly." He nuzzled her cheek gently. "And you have too, haven't you? It isn't just that you can see me, and hear me talking, you can do magic spells. I'm sure I can feel it in you."

Molly blushed, and nodded. "I've only ever done one spell on my own," she explained. "That was bewitching some daisy petals." Molly explained about Snowdrop, the mischievous vanishing rabbit. "And I did spells with a witch's kitten called Sparkle, too, and with Star and Stella, the wish puppies."

Molly smiled dreamily to herself,

 remembering the wonderful feeling of magic fizzing through her body as she helped with the spells. Then all at once she looked up, worriedly. "Silver, I've

just had an awful thought. You need to hide! If you stay here, someone's bound to notice you, and send you back to Mrs James. I bet she'll call the police, and put signs up, all that sort of thing."

Silver nodded. "I know. I must go back home, but it's a long journey, and difficult. I need a little time to rest before I set off, just a few days to get strong again. Being shut away in that stable has left me weak."

Molly frowned. "I'd love it if you could stay here, but the orchard is so close to the house. My mum and dad and Kitty — that's my little sister — they all go past here every day. One of them would be bound to spot you. You can't turn invisible or anything like that, can you?" she added, thinking of Snowdrop the rabbit.

Silver snorted a horsy laugh. "No, I'm afraid not. But I do have an idea, and I think you might be able to help. Climb up on my back, Molly."

Molly hesitated. "Are you sure?" Somehow it felt very special to ride a unicorn, as though it was something that only princesses, or fairies, ought to be allowed to do.

Silver snorted again, and nudged her with his nose. "Of course, silly. I want you to. Besides, I need you to help me with the spell."

Molly smiled at him shyly. "I'd love to." She climbed up a couple more rungs of the gate, and carefully threw her leg over Silver's back. She'd ridden bareback once at the stables, but Silver was much more slender and graceful than dear old Whisky, who was like riding a table. She wriggled experimentally to see how well she could stay on, but Silver shook his mane, and tossed his head. "That tickles! Don't worry, Molly, I won't let you fall."

Molly patted his neck gently. "I don't feel like I *could* fall," she admitted. It was as though she and Silver had been joined into one person. She could sense the magic racing all round his body, and now she was part of it too.

"Good." Silver set off at a walk round the orchard, looking carefully at the trees. "I shall know when I come to the right place," he muttered. "Ah! This – this is perfect." He was standing by Molly's favourite apple tree, a big old one which was easy to climb, and had the most delicious sweet, crunchy apples. "Hold on tight," Silver told her, looking back over his shoulder.

Molly leaned forward and hugged him tightly round the neck, and Silver started to walk slowly backwards around the tree, lowering his head so that his horn drew a magical circle in the dewy grass. The circle flared silver, glowing and sparkling in the sunlight, and Molly's fingers glittered as her magic joined the circle too.

When he had gone all the way round the tree, Silver stepped inside the circle and Molly slipped from his back. They looked at it delightedly. "That is *very* good," Silver told her with a little whinny of pleasure. "Your magic works beautifully with mine. Now, only we two will be able to enter this circle, and when we're in it, no one will be able to see us. I can hide here and rest for as long as I need."

Molly stared admiringly at the circle, and then she gasped. "Silver, look! The apples!"

Silver looked up into the tree where she was pointing. The last few apples at the top of the tree were shining softly silver too.

"Aren't they beautiful?" Molly breathed softly, and Silver rubbed his head fondly against her shoulder. Molly patted his velvety nose. "Your magic is amazing, Silver. You're so clever. I never knew unicorns could do spells."

Silver looked pleased. "Well, mostly we're known for healing. Our horns can heal wounds, you know, or cure people who've been poisoned."

"Wow," Molly whispered. "That's really special."

Silver stared sadly over her shoulder, looking into the distance. "It is a wonderful gift," he agreed. "But we can hardly ever use it."

"Why not?" Molly frowned, puzzled. "Is it very difficult to do? I suppose it is. I should think it would wear you out, healing people."

Silver's head drooped. "No, it's hard, but not too hard. It's because once I cure someone, Molly, they know what I am. Oh, sometimes we can do it secretly. But that's very difficult."

"And once they know what you are..." Molly said thoughtfully.

"Once they know what I am, Molly, they want me to belong to them. So they can use my magic for themselves. Some people would even steal our horns."

"You mean, cut them off?" Molly gasped in horror.

Silver nodded, closing his eyes and shuddering at the idea.

"That's awful," Molly whispered.

"Would it ... grow back?"

"Eventually. But it would be very painful." Silver stared anxiously at his horn, which meant he went rather cross-eyed.

Molly leaned against the gate, thinking hard. "My dad is a vet, did you know that? He heals animals, that's his job."

Silver shook his mane. "I didn't know. He must be very special."

"Oh, he is!" Molly agreed. "I was

just thinking, though. I know he'd love to have magical healing powers, but I don't think he'd ever steal a unicorn horn. In fact, I'm sure he wouldn't."

Silver sighed. "It's hard to know who to trust. I'm sure you're right about your father, but if he found a unicorn in his garden, what would he do?"

Molly looked doubtful. "I'm not sure. Maybe tell lots of other vets? I should think they'd all want to see you. They'd be amazed!"

"And would you trust every one of these other vets, and all the people they would tell?"

"Oh..." Molly shook her head slightly. "No. No, I suppose not. I see what you mean."

"I can only tell people that I can trust to keep my secret," Silver told her gently.

"I won't tell *anyone!*" Molly promised. It was a little frightening to have such an important secret. Then she sighed.

"What is it? Are you wishing you hadn't found me?" Silver asked anxiously.

"Oh, no!" Molly assured him. "I just wish that you *could* use your healing powers here, that's all. My dad has a cat at the surgery at the moment, she was hit by a car, and she's very ill. He did a big operation on her on Saturday, the morning I met you at Grandad's forge, but she's not doing very well..."

Silver's ears pricked forward interestedly. "I could try to help. If the cat doesn't get better, perhaps we could do it without your father knowing. I've never tried to heal a cat, but I'm sure I could."

Molly flung her arms around the unicorn's neck. It felt like hugging any other pony, except for the wonderful fizzing, sparkling sensation that rushed through her as she buried her face in his mane, and whispered, "Oh, thank you, Silver!"

Chapter Five

Alice's Story

Molly stayed hugging Silver for what seemed like ages. The wonderful magic in his mane made her feel so happy and strong.

"My dad would be so pleased if we could help Sasha," she whispered hopefully. Then she gasped and looked up. "My dad! Oh, Silver, what time is it? We've been here ages. Mum and Dad will be getting up soon, and they'll wonder where I am. I'd better go. Will you be all right here on your own?"

Silver nodded. "Of course you must go. But you will visit me later, won't you?" he asked wistfully.

"As soon as I get back from school," Molly promised. She gave him a quick kiss on the nose, and raced back to the gate, scrambling over and making a dash for the house. "Oh no," she muttered, as she saw her dad sitting at the kitchen table. She'd hoped she'd be able to get in before her parents noticed she was gone. Molly shut the back door behind with a soft click, and waited for her dad to ask her where on earth she'd been.

He didn't. He took a sip of his coffee, and smiled sadly at her. "Hi Molly," he murmured.

Molly stared at him. Not even one

question about why she was outside?
Molly looked at the kitchen clock. It
was only six-thirty. Well, that was good,
because Mum probably hadn't tried to
wake her up yet. But why was Dad so
dopey? And why was he in the kitchen at
half-past six in the morning? Usually he
liked his sleep.

"Is everything OK, Dad?" Molly asked
worriedly.

Her dad shook his head. "I just went to check on Sasha, the hit-and-run cat. She's not doing well, Molly. I'm thinking we might lose her. It's just such a shame."

"Oh, Dad..." Molly breathed.

"She's such a friendly little thing. I've had her in the surgery for vaccinations and everyday stuff. And her owners – two little girls, Molly, they're going to be devastated." Dad stared across the room, frowning. "I've tried everything, Molly. I'm just not sure what else I can do..."

Molly caught her breath. Maybe there wasn't much else Dad could do for Sasha, but there *was* something she could do. If only she could get Silver into the surgery...

Molly was very silent on the walk to school, as she tried to work out some way of getting Sasha and Silver together. She waved goodbye to Mum and Kitty at the gates to the nursery, and walked slowly on to the school entrance, not bothering to run in after her friends like she usually would.

As she turned into the gates, a car drew up. Molly ducked behind the gatepost when she saw Mrs James get out. She really didn't want Silver's owner to see her right now! She just couldn't like her – she wasn't sure how Mrs James had managed to have a daughter as nice as Alice.

Mrs James seemed just as cross as she had on Saturday. "Hurry up, Alice! Don't forget your recorder!"

Alice obediently hustled herself out of the car, laden with bags and her coat.

"I'm going off to the police station now, to tell them about the pony. Who knows if we'll ever hear anything..." Mrs James muttered.

Alice nodded. "Bye Mum," she called quietly, as Mrs James got into the car, and she waved her recorder. Alice watched the car go off round the corner, and sighed. Then she turned and looked at the playground, full of people chatting, or racing about, and she sighed again, and walked very slowly in. She sat down on one of the benches, and looked wistfully at a group of girls from their class talking.

Molly was very tempted to go and talk to her – she really wanted to know what Alice thought of Silver, whether she had any idea what he really was – but the bell went, and they had to hurry into school.

But at lunch time, Molly sat down nervously next to Alice.

She was on that same bench again. Alice gave her a shy smile, and Molly smiled back. She took a deep breath. Alice had seemed nice when she'd spoken to her a couple of times before, but Molly was still a little nervous.

"I was walking past you this morning, and I'm really sorry, but I couldn't help hearing your mum say she was going to the police about your pony. Is he all right?"

Alice shook her head sadly. "I don't know. He's gone."

"Oh no – do you think he's been stolen?" Molly asked, crossing her fingers under her skirt and feeling guilty. "That's awful. You must be really upset."

Alice looked thoughtfully at Molly, then lowered her voice to a whisper. "I let him go."

"What?" Molly squeaked. She certainly

hadn't been expecting that.

"I left the bolt on the stable door undone. I stuck a piece of paper in the door, so it looked closed." Alice stared at her fingers.

"*Why?*" Molly asked her disbelievingly.

Alice looked up at her. "He wasn't happy," she murmured. "I don't like riding any more and I don't know an awful lot about ponies, but even I could see that.

Maybe I could tell because I'm not very happy either," she added quietly. "He just kept staring out of the stable door, looking out across the field to the woods, as though he was desperate to get away. It looked like he wanted to go home. I know how he felt. So I let him go."

Alice blinked. "But I wish I hadn't. He might not have been able to find his way back there. What if he's been hurt on the road somewhere?" She sniffed. "And I really miss him. He was so lovely. Even though I didn't want to ride him, I loved brushing him, and stroking his mane."

She smiled a shy smile at Molly. "He had the most gorgeous mane, you wouldn't believe. Just stroking it made me feel all sparkly and happy. You probably think I'm being stupid," she said defensively.

Molly shook her head. "No, I believe you," she said earnestly. "I really do. Some animals are like that." It was all she could say without giving away too much of the truth, but it seemed to help Alice.

"Thanks," Alice murmured, blowing her nose. "I'm glad I told you. You won't tell anyone else, will you?" she asked, suddenly anxious.

Molly shook her head. She *was* planning to tell someone what Alice had said, but she didn't think Alice would mind...

Molly crept out of the house while Mum was reading a story to Kitty that afternoon after school. Mum probably thought she was doing her homework, but this was a lot more important. She raced over to the orchard, and clambered over the gate.

Silver looked up anxiously as he heard her running across the grass. When he saw it was Molly, he gave a delighted whinny.

Molly stepped into the enchanted circle, shivering a little as the magic sparkled over her from top to toe. She hugged Silver, and he breathed sweet horsy breath down her neck.

Molly giggled. Then she said thoughtfully, "You know, Silver, I think Alice could feel your magic too."

Silver looked up eagerly. "You saw her? How is she? Was she missing me? I worry about her, she seemed so lonely."

Molly nodded. "*Very* lonely. She's really worried about you too. I think you were her only friend, Silver. And she still let you go."

Silver drew in a sharp breath. "You mean — *she* left the stable unbolted?"

"On purpose. She said you kept staring out at the woods like you were desperate to go home. And she knew how you felt, so she let you go." Molly's voice shook a little. It had been so brave of Alice.

Silver looked out across the orchard, his dark blue eyes troubled. "I've been thinking about this all day," he said at last. "We have to tell Alice where I am. We've got to trust her. She cared enough to give me my freedom. She deserves to know I'm safe."

Chapter Six

The Magic Apples

"I've been worrying about something else too," Silver told Molly, his tail flicking from side to side. "I can feel a sick creature nearby. Very sick, Molly. Whoever it is – I don't think they have much time left. But I'm sure I could help." His tail twitched anxiously, faster and faster, and Molly stroked his neck soothingly.

"I think it's Sasha you can feel," she explained. "The cat I told you about before. My dad says she's really sick, and he's worried he might lose her." She leaned her head against Silver's neck. "I just don't see how I can get you close enough to Sasha to heal her," she said, tearing a leaf into tiny pieces crossly. "I can't bring her out here, I'd never get her out without someone seeing us, and she's just too sick, anyway. Oh, what are we going to do? We can't just let her fade away!"

Molly stared up into the tree, blinking back tears. Shimmering high above her, the silver apples floated against the blue sky. Molly nibbled her lip thoughtfully. "Silver?" she asked at last. "Why did the apples change colour? After we made the magic circle, I mean?"

Silver looked up too. "I should think that some of our magic went into the ground, and up through the tree roots to the apples," he answered, not really paying attention. Then his furry ears pricked forward with sudden understanding. "Our magic is in the apples... Molly!"

"Do you think it will work?" Molly asked eagerly.

"Let's try! Climb up on my back, then you should be able to reach one." Silver moved as close as he could towards the tree, so that Molly could clamber up.

Standing on tiptoe on his back, gripping on to the trunk, Molly stretched up into the tree, her fingertips just touching an apple. Its skin was smooth and silky, and it pulsed with magic as her fingers brushed against it.

139

"I shall rear a little," Silver warned her. "Hold tight. You should be able to reach – now!" Effortlessly he lifted his front hooves from the ground, and Molly gasped and grabbed the apple, sliding down on to Silver's back with a rustle of leaves.

"Are you all right?" Silver asked, nosing round at her anxiously.

"I think so!" Molly told him. Luckily she had her thick jacket on which had protected her. She gazed at the apple. It *looked* magical. It was still apple-coloured, but somehow it was silver as well. Not a cold, metallic silver, but a rich soft glowing colour. It smelled gorgeous too. Cats didn't normally like apples, but she was sure that even a cat would try this one.

"Hurry, Molly," Silver told her anxiously. "Go and try!"

Molly nodded, and slipped down from his back. She hurried over to the surgery. Luckily no one was in reception, and she crept quietly into the ward area.

Sasha was lying on her side in one of the cages. She was hardly even breathing, and one of her eyes was half open, and looked dull and grey. Molly gulped. Could anything save her? She had to try. She dug a tiny piece of apple out with her fingernail, and poked it through the wire. The apple was full of silvery, sweet-smelling juice. It dripped from Molly's finger on to Sasha's bluish mouth.

Nothing happened.

Then, very slowly, Sasha's tongue moved to lick the apple juice from the corner of her mouth.

Molly hurriedly pushed the rest of the

tiny piece of apple between her teeth, and
Sasha's eyelids fluttered.

It was working!

After watching Sasha for a few more
moments, Molly sneaked quietly out of
the surgery again. She was intending to
go back to the orchard to tell Silver that
she thought the apple had started
to work.

But when she came round the corner of the surgery, she discovered that there was no need to go to the orchard. Silver was already there. With Grandad.

Molly gulped.

I wanted to see if it had worked! Silver said anxiously in her head. *I was watching through the window. I think it will cure her, but we'll have to give it time. And . . . I'm afraid we may have a small problem. . .*

Molly gazed speechlessly at them, thinking that actually Grandad looked to her like rather a big problem.

"Molly, this is Mrs James's pony, isn't it?" Grandad asked, sounding rather puzzled.

"Um, yes. . ." Molly admitted.

NO! Silver shouted silently, and Molly winced. That hurt.

"I mean, no. . . He was kidnapped. . ." Molly muttered, trying to think of a way to explain that didn't involve unicorns.

"But Ellie at the riding school told me that Mrs James has reported him to the police as stolen! Has he been here all the time?" Grandad asked worriedly.

At this point, Silver took two steps closer to Grandad, and butted his head into Grandad's shoulder, obviously asking to be given some attention. Grandad stroked his mane absent-mindedly. "Yes, you're very lovely," he murmured. "But Molly, we need to sort this out..." Grandad blinked, and then shook his head. "What was I saying?"

Molly smiled to herself as she saw the silver sparkles rising out of Silver's mane, and wafting round Grandad. Silver had bewitched him, so that Grandad had forgotten that this was a stolen pony, and even that Molly shouldn't have a pony in the yard at all!

"I still think there's something very odd about this pony," Grandad said thoughtfully, looking at Silver's forehead. "Something I can't quite put my finger on..."

Silver gazed at him innocently, trying to look ever so normal, and spoke in Molly's mind. *Your grandfather can almost see I'm a unicorn, Molly. He isn't quite as magical as you, but nearly. I think you could trust him*

to help you, if you should ever need to.

Molly nodded. "I'm going to take Silver back now," she said hesitantly, not sure how Grandad would react.

"Yes, yes, of course," Grandad murmured, still staring unseeingly at Silver's horn. "I hope I'll see him again, he's a beautiful creature." And he turned, and wandered away round the front of the surgery.

"Wow! Your magic is really strong!" Molly told Silver admiringly. "That was amazing – and I'm sure Sasha is starting to get better, did you see her? She had her eyes open, just for a minute, and then she fell asleep again, but it was different sleep. Her breathing was stronger, and I really think her fur was glossier too. We'll just have to wait and see."

Silver pawed the ground shyly. "I'm glad it worked. And I'm sorry I came out of the circle – I just wanted to see." Then he sighed. "Now all we need to do is help Alice. But I think that could be the hardest job of all."

Molly waited for Alice at the gate the next morning – she was hoping that if she could persuade her to come to tea, Alice could ask her mother right then. Molly had already asked Mum, who thought it was a lovely idea, especially when Alice didn't know many people yet. She promised that she would be sure to have enough tea in case Alice was able to come.

As soon as Alice's car pulled up, Molly ran over to her, and smiled politely at Mrs James. Mrs James frowned slightly –

she obviously remembered who Molly was, but she looked pleased when Molly invited Alice round. Molly looked hopefully at Alice. *Please say yes!* she told her silently, wishing she could really talk in people's minds, like Silver could.

"Oh!" Alice sounded delighted. "Oh, yes, please!" And she beamed at Molly, looking less shy than Molly had ever seen her. They went on into school together, chatting happily about how awful their science homework was.

After school, Alice walked back home with Molly and Mum and Kitty. Mum was really happy, and told them all that the poor cat in the surgery had started to get better. Molly smiled to herself. Silver had done it! And she had helped him!

Mum got them all some raisins to

nibble on while they were waiting for tea,
and persuaded Kitty to help her cook.

She gave Molly and Alice a smiling look,
which meant that she knew they didn't
want Kitty hanging around, and suggested
that Molly showed Alice round outside.
Molly agreed delightedly – she'd been
wondering how they'd get out to see
Silver without Kitty.

"Come and see the orchard," she suggested to Alice. "There's some really good trees to climb."

They leaned on the orchard gate together, Alice telling Molly about her old house. Molly wasn't really listening. She was peering through the trees, hoping that Silver would hear them. *Silver, Alice is here!* she called to him. *Come out!*

Silver came stepping silently through the trees. Molly thought he looked anxious, as though he was worried how Alice might react to seeing him. He needn't have been. Alice gasped, then scrambled over the gate so fast she fell, though she didn't seem to care about her scraped knees. She raced across the grass to Silver, and hugged him, burying her face in his mane, while he nuzzled at her delightedly.

Molly followed her slowly, wanting to give them some time alone together. As she came closer, Alice looked up. "You found him!" she said, her eyes shining.

Molly nodded. "He turned up here on Monday. That's why I asked you about him at school. I'm sorry, I didn't know who he belonged to." It was *almost* true.

I don't belong to anyone! Silver tossed his head, and his voice in Molly's mind was stern.

Alice looked up at him, blinking. She looked confused, and Molly wondered how much she could see.

"I don't think he's mine, Molly," she said hesitantly. "I think he's got somewhere else to go. I wish he'd stay with me, I've missed him so much, but I want him to be happy. I'm just pleased to know he's safe." She sighed. "I – I almost think I could ride him. I fell off at my riding school last year, and I broke my leg, really badly. Mum bought me Silver to try and persuade me to ride again, but I didn't want to. He's so gentle though. I'm sure he wouldn't let me fall. . ." She gazed at Silver lovingly.

Then she gulped, and turned bravely to Molly. "Maybe if he stays here, could I come and visit him sometimes? This is such a beautiful place, I can see why he'd want to stay. It's almost magical, isn't it?" She looked round at the trees, their leaves turning golden in the autumn sun.

"I think he has to go," Molly said sadly. "He doesn't really belong here."

I could stay, Silver told her silently, and Molly looked up at him in surprise. *I do like it, being with people. It's interesting. And she needs me. If she promises never to put iron shoes on me, I'll stay.*

Molly looked thoughtfully at Alice. How was she going to explain that? Alice was still leaning lovingly against Silver's shoulder, her fingers twisted in his mane. Molly gave Silver a meaningful look, and

he snorted in agreement. A silver glow
wrapped softly around Alice, making
her sigh happily, her eyelashes fluttering
against her cheeks. She nodded, as if she
understood something very important.

"Could your grandad make silver
horseshoes?" she murmured to Molly.
Molly smiled. "I'm sure he could."

If he does, Silver said happily, *I'll still be a unicorn, but I'll be Alice's unicorn, and she'll be able to ride me.*

Molly stroked his velvety nose, and sighed. It was the happiest ending she could have wished for.

One day soon, she was sure, she would have her own pet to love, just as much as Alice loved Silver.

Read more about Molly's
magical adventures!

The girl who talks to animals

Magic Molly

The Witch's Kitten

HOLLY WEBB

The girl who talks to animals

Magic Molly

The Wish Puppy

HOLLY WEBB

The girl who talks to animals
Magic Molly
The Good Luck Duck
HOLLY WEBB

The girl who talks to animals
Magic Molly
The Shy Piglet
HOLLY WEBB

Look out for more
by Holly Webb

A
Cat Called
PENGUIN

HOLLY WEBB
Illustrated by Polly Dunbar

The
CHOCOLATE
Dog

HOLLY WEBB
Illustrated by Sharon Rentta

HOLLY WEBB has always loved animals. As a child she had two dogs, a cat, and at one point, nine gerbils (an accident). Holly's other love is books. Holly lives in Reading with her husband, three sons and a very spoilt cat.

www.holly-webb.com

10 Quick Questions for Holly Webb

1. Kittens or puppies? Kittens

2. Chocolate or Sweets? Chocolate

3. Salad or chips? Chips

4. Favourite websites? Youtube, Lolcats

5. Text or call? Call

6. Favourite lesson at school? Ancient Greek (you did ask...)

7. Worst lesson at school? Physics

8. Favourite colour? Green

9. Favourite film? *The Sound of Music*

10. City or countryside? Countryside, but with fast trains to the city!